Date Due

E
Tho

Thomas' railway word book

THOMAS'
Railway Word Book

Illustrated by Paul Nichols

bird

dome

whistle

tender

wheel arch

Random House 🏠 New York

A Random House PICTUREBACK® Book

Britt Allcroft's Thomas & Friends based on The Railway Series by The Rev W Awdry.
Copyright © Britt Allcroft (Thomas) LLC 2000. THOMAS & FRIENDS is a trademark of Britt Allcroft Inc
in the USA, Mexico and Canada and of Britt Allcroft (Thomas) Limited in the rest of the world.
THE BRITT ALLCROFT COMPANY is a trademark of The Britt Allcroft Company plc.
All rights reserved under International and Pan-American Copyright Conventions. Published in the United States
by Random House, Inc., New York, and simultaneously in Canada by Random House of Canada Limited, Toronto.
www.randomhouse.com/kids   www.thomasthetankengine.com
ISBN 0-375-80281-9
Library of Congress Catalog Card Number: 00-100733
Printed in the United States of America   November 2000   10 9 8 7 6 5 4 3 2 1

porthole

logs

Percy pushes a **freight car** to James.
James' **coupling hook** connects to the **coupling chain**.

coupling hook

buffer

5

ht car

coupling chain

James holds coal in a special bin called a **tender**.
He uses his **whistle** to talk to a **bird**.

dome

whistle

bird

top hat

tender

tree

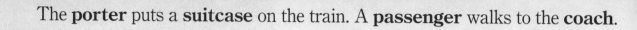

The **porter** puts a **suitcase** on the train. A **passenger** walks to the **coach**.

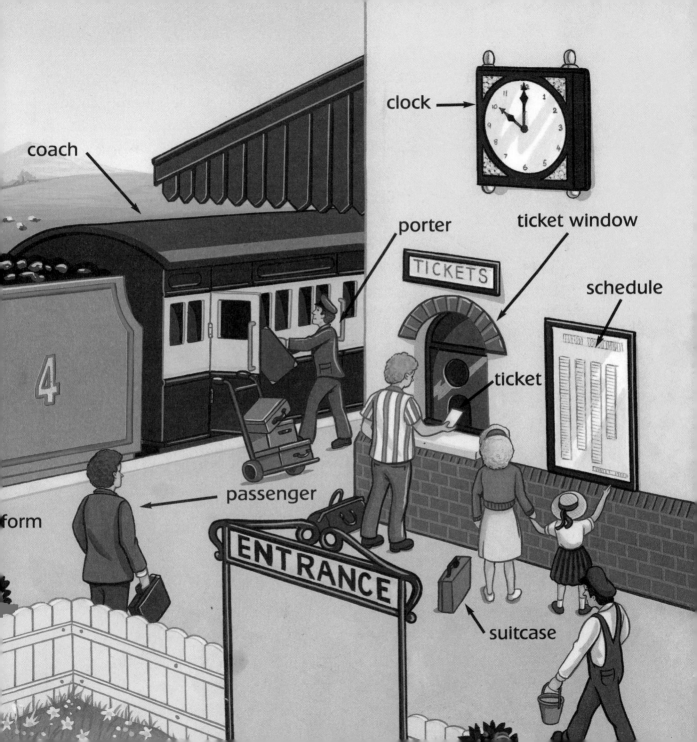

coach

clock

porter

ticket window

TICKETS

schedule

ticket

form

passenger

ENTRANCE

4

suitcase

Henry has had an accident.
The **breakdown train** uses a **crane** to lift Henry back onto the track.

hook

sheep

hay bale

flatbed car

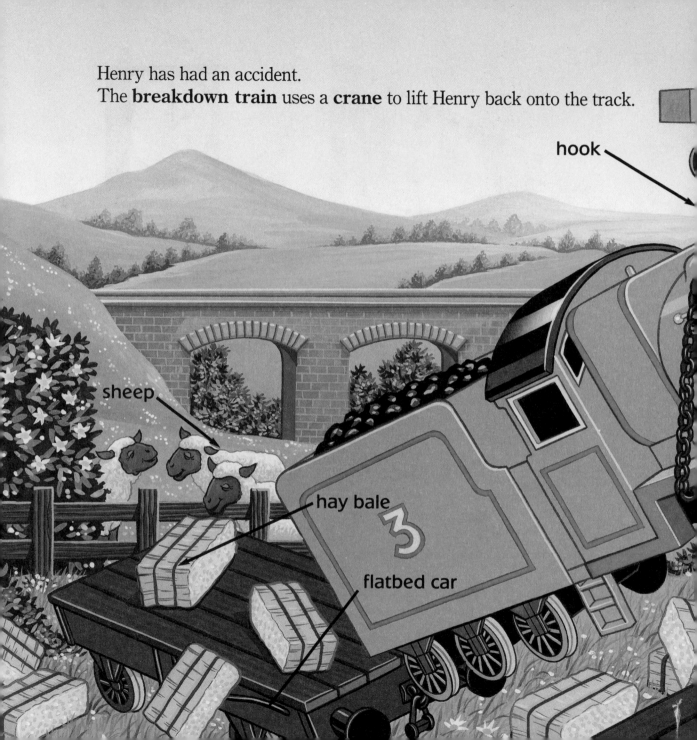

smoke

Thomas crosses the **viaduct** over the **river**.
His **driver** waves to the people in the **house**.

chimney

viaduct

river

house

Snow makes Thomas' **wheels** slip.
He uses his **snowplow** to clear the **tracks**.

mountain

snow

nowplow

Mavis and Thomas meet at the junction.
Mavis is a **diesel engine** pulling a load of **gravel**.

flag

guard

steps

gravel

signal

diesel engine

MAVIS

THE FFARQUHAR QUARRY CO. LTD.

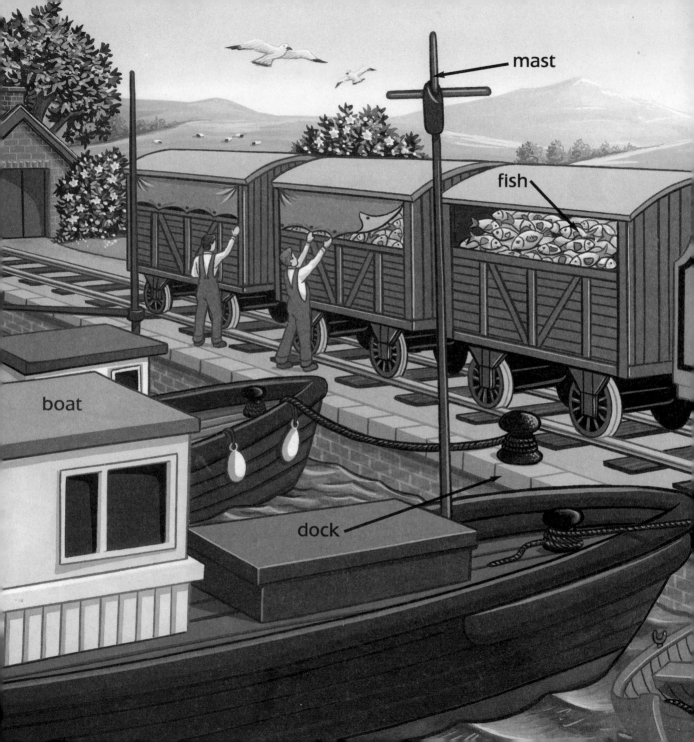

mast

fish

boat

dock

James picks up **fish** at the **dock**.
A **sailor** ties up his **boat** with a strong **rope**.

helicopter

or

rope

seagull

steam

ladder

Thomas' tank is filled with **water**
from the **water tower**.

water tower

water

pipe

1

wheel arch

Toby is an old-fashioned **tram engine**.
Instead of a whistle, he has a **bell**.

cow

bus

tram engine

wooden panel

bell

7

cowcatcher

Gordon spins around on the **turntable**.

fence

funnel

handrail

turntable

The trains rest in the **shed** at night.

moon

shed

star

omas

James

Henry

Percy

Gordon

Thomas' **lamp** sits on his **lamp rod**. Good night, Thomas.

lamp rod

lamp

brake pipe